THE
HOUSE *of*
WISDOM

A MELANIE KROUPA BOOK

THE HOUSE of WISDOM

FLORENCE PARRY HEIDE
& JUDITH HEIDE GILLILAND

ILLUSTRATED BY MARY GRANDPRÉ

A DK INK BOOK

DK PUBLISHING, INC.

FROM TIME TO TIME, as the world turns, something different happens, something mysterious and astonishing: a kind of brightening, a quickening, a leap beyond, when ideas brush against one another and sparks fly and ignite other ideas. It can happen anywhere, anytime.

It happened in Babylonia, long ago, and in Egypt. It happened in Greece. No one knows why it starts, or why it ends, but the echoes of it last and last.

A brightening like this happened a thousand years ago in Baghdad.

Baghdad, in those times, was a great city, the prince of all cities. Even in the farthest reaches of the world people knew of Baghdad. Like a silent voice calling, like an invisible thread pulling, it gathered to itself all that the world had to offer.

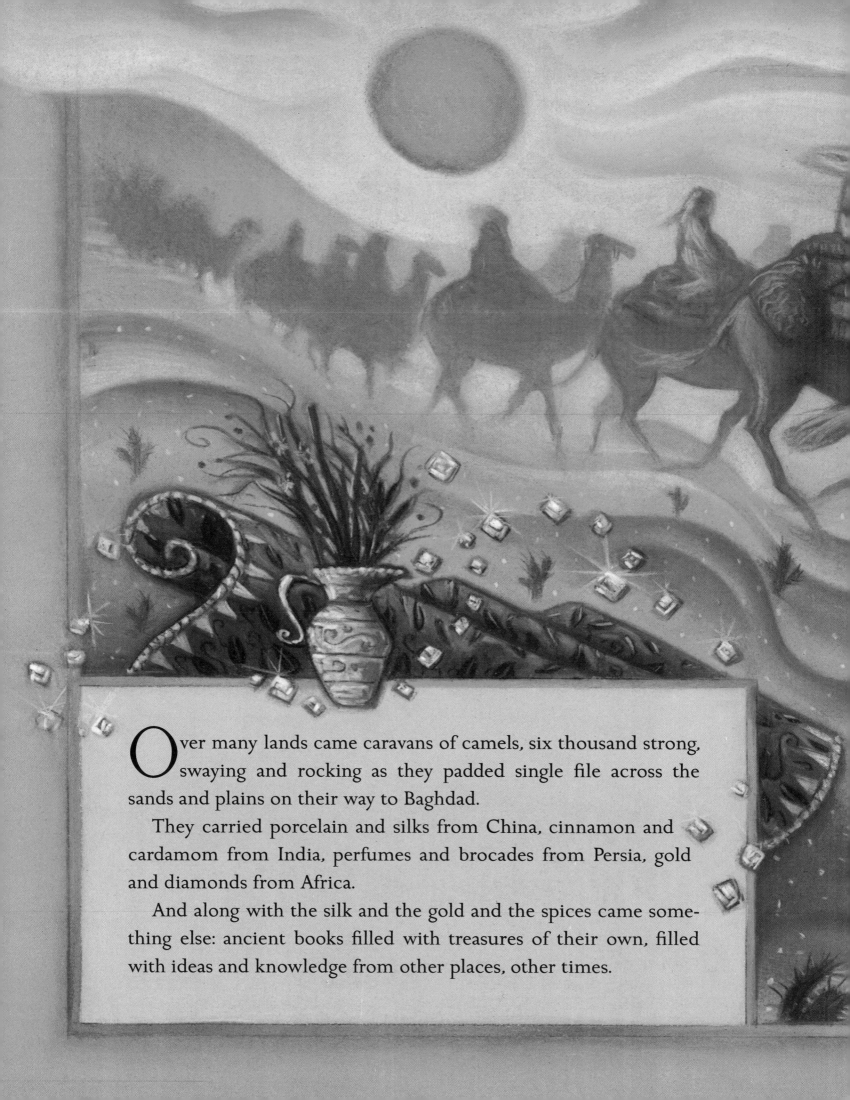

Over many lands came caravans of camels, six thousand strong, swaying and rocking as they padded single file across the sands and plains on their way to Baghdad.

They carried porcelain and silks from China, cinnamon and cardamom from India, perfumes and brocades from Persia, gold and diamonds from Africa.

And along with the silk and the gold and the spices came something else: ancient books filled with treasures of their own, filled with ideas and knowledge from other places, other times.

The caravans came. The dust rose and the sun burned, and still they came.

And across seas and up rivers and into the crowded harbor of Baghdad sailed ships, ships of all kinds, some shaped like dolphins, some like eagles, some like lions. They came carrying fragrant musk and brilliant dyes, rubies and lapis lazuli, pearls and daggers.

And with these treasures came the other riches, the books and manuscripts from far and forgotten times.

The ships came. The winds blew and the waves crashed, and still they came.

Now the ruler of Baghdad at that time was the Caliph al-Ma'mun. He enjoyed his riches and everything that his gold could buy. But of all the treasures that came to Baghdad by land and by sea, he most valued the books.

He built a great library to hold them, and he called it the House of Wisdom. But it was more than a house, it was more than a library, it was more even than a palace. It was the very center of the brightening that was Baghdad.

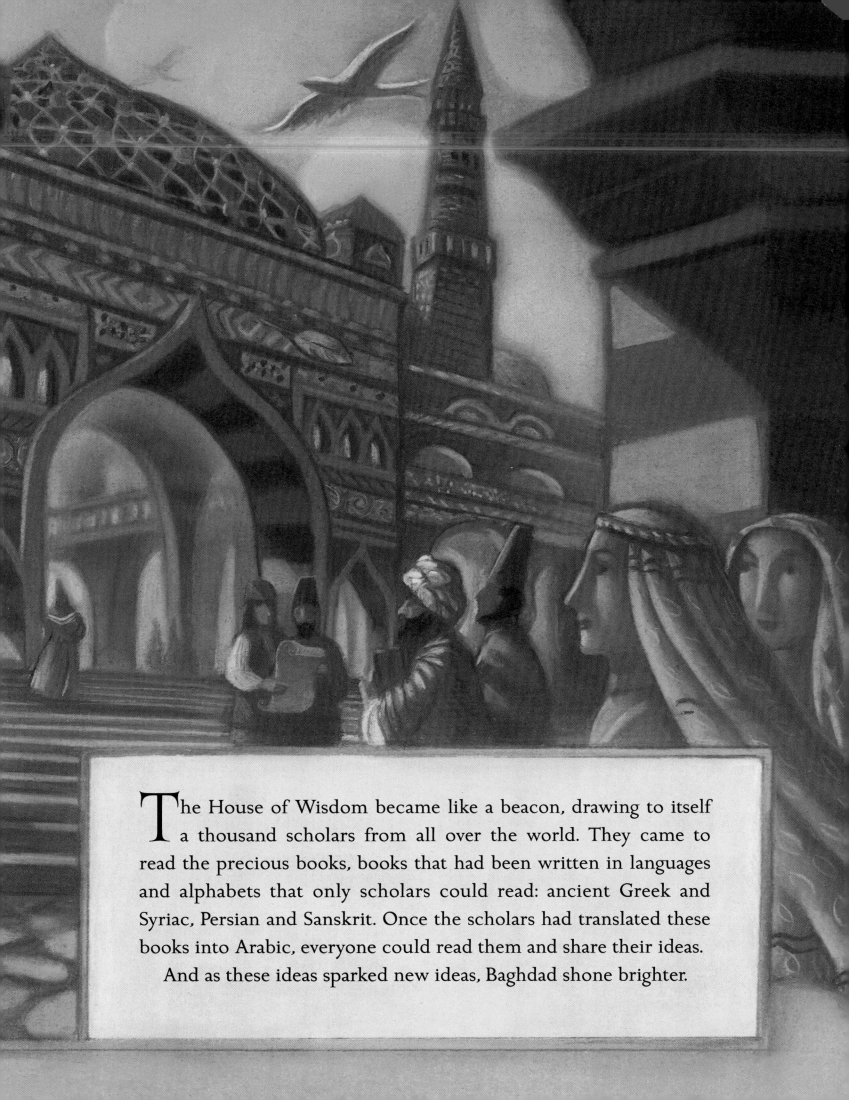

The House of Wisdom became like a beacon, drawing to itself a thousand scholars from all over the world. They came to read the precious books, books that had been written in languages and alphabets that only scholars could read: ancient Greek and Syriac, Persian and Sanskrit. Once the scholars had translated these books into Arabic, everyone could read them and share their ideas. And as these ideas sparked new ideas, Baghdad shone brighter.

Here in the House of Wisdom, a boy named Ishaq lived with his father and his mother. Often he explored the hundreds of rooms and courtyards of this great library, chasing his shadow through the hallways and up and down the wide marble stairs, looking into the many rooms filled with shelves of books and wondering at the still, quiet scholars bent over their studies.

shaq's father, Hunayn, worked all day at his books. He was the best translator in all of Baghdad. The Caliph himself so prized Hunayn's translations that for each completed manuscript, the Caliph gave him its equal weight in gold. But Ishaq knew it was not the gold that was important to his father. It was something else, something that could not be weighed or touched or measured or found even in Baghdad's famous market.

The souk, Baghdad's crowded marketplace, offered almost everything imaginable. It seemed that all the world came there to
buy and sell. Ishaq watched the crowds of people from faraway
places with curiosity: Russian traders in fur caps, Indians in white
dhotis, Turks in billowing pantaloons, Africans in brilliant orange
robes. They spoke in languages he had never heard.

"They speak so strangely," Ishaq whispered one day.

"You may not understand them, but that does not mean they
have nothing to say," said Hunayn.

Later that night Ishaq looked for his father and found him in his study, reading a manuscript in Greek.

"You are so often alone here, Father," he said.

Hunayn smiled and touched the book before him. "I am never alone. I am with Aristotle, who reaches out to me across time and shows us how to search for the answers. That searching is the great adventure; it is the fire in our hearts."

"But he lived a thousand years ago. People did not know much then," Ishaq said. "They were not like us."

"They were not so different," said Hunayn. "And the ones who come after us will not be so different either. We are like leaves of the same tree, separated by many autumns."

When Ishaq left his father's study, he climbed the stairs around and around and up and up to his favorite room. There the scholars studied the stars and measured the earth. Aristotle would have looked at these same stars a thousand years ago. And someday someone in the future would look at them and wonder too. "Maybe it is only time that separates us," he thought. There was so much to know.

"I want to be a man of learning," he decided. "Like my father. Like Aristotle."

And so, many mornings Ishaq sat with his books, reading the ancient Greek words one at a time, then writing them in Arabic, slowly. How different it was when he threw the javelin, when he raced his horse, or when he hunted the wild boar with the cheetah. Then the time flew! But studying was long, difficult, slow work.

He thought of his father's joy when a special manuscript had come to him through time and distance, by camel and by ship. How could ancient words mean so much? Yes, he wanted to be a scholar, but he also wanted to travel, to explore the world.

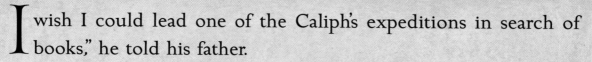

I wish I could lead one of the Caliph's expeditions in search of books," he told his father.

"One day you will; seeing the world is part of becoming a learned man. But first you must study, you must prepare yourself, you must make room in your head and in your heart for all you will see."

So Ishaq studied, he read, he translated. He became a good student, even a scholar. He learned about astronomy and mathematics, about geography and medicine. He studied the writings of ancient Greek thinkers such as Galen and Plato and Hippocrates.

But still he did not feel the fire.

And then one day the Caliph chose Ishaq to lead an expedition to search for books. Now he could explore! At last he would see the world.

His father went with him to the great caravansary, where the drivers and their camels had gathered in preparation for the long journey. He embraced Ishaq. "On your travels you will learn much—from the storyteller in rags, from the birds, from the stars. It will all become part of you."

Ishaq rode by camel and horse through desert and plain, along well-traveled roads and desolate trails. He sailed from river to sea and from port to port.

He listened to the trumpeting of elephants beside the Ganges and talked with learned scholars in fragrant gardens in Persia. He hunted the crocodile along the Nile and wrapped himself against fierce sandstorms in the Sahara.

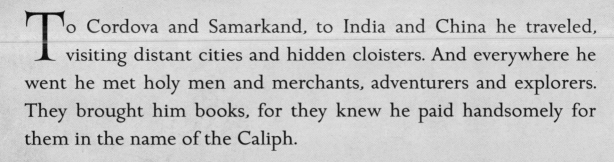

To Cordova and Samarkand, to India and China he traveled, visiting distant cities and hidden cloisters. And everywhere he went he met holy men and merchants, adventurers and explorers. They brought him books, for they knew he paid handsomely for them in the name of the Caliph.

Everything he saw and heard and felt was new and strange, but for the rising of the sun each day and the canopy of stars at night.

In Athens he walked the streets that Aristotle had once walked. He thought of Aristotle surrounded by students. For a moment he imagined he was one of them, and felt a quickening in his mind. Maybe the ideas they shared, the excitement they felt, could reach across time.

He traveled even to the west, to the dark, ruined land of the barbarians. Here the people believed in witches and demons, in spells and charms. In this land scarcely anyone could read or write. But hidden away in hills and forests and caves there lived quiet, robed monks who spent their days copying old books, saving what little wisdom and learning they could in those dark times.

Ishaq thought of the thousand scholars bent over their books in the House of Wisdom, their lanterns shining deep into the night. He longed for home.

But he continued his journey, everywhere gathering more books. There were so many books and manuscripts that Ishaq could not know them all, armfuls and basketfuls of books of all kinds, pages of books, pieces of books, old and forgotten books.

For three years he traveled the world.

At last it was time to return home to Baghdad. He wondered if he was now ready to live the life of a scholar.

As his ship finally entered the harbor of Baghdad one summer night, Ishaq looked to the House of Wisdom on the hillside. It seemed to him that the lights of the scholars' lanterns were like new stars that had come close to earth, and that the glow of those lanterns might reach to the darkness of the land he had seen.

Ishaq saw his father and mother waiting on the dock, and he hurried to meet them. They embraced for a long time.

Hunayn looked into Ishaq's eyes. "You have grown in many ways, my son."

"I have learned many things, father. But come and see what I have brought you," Ishaq said proudly. "Manuscripts from Damascus and Alexandria, from Aleppo and Constantinople and Tripoli. Hundreds and hundreds, father, thousands and thousands!"

They hurried to the head of the long procession of servants carrying the baskets of manuscripts, a chain of books that stretched from the harbor to the very doors of the House of Wisdom.

The scholars awaiting them greeted Ishaq and the books like old friends and celebrated their arrival with joy.

The Great Room had been emptied for these new treasures. The scholars, men and women, gathered around, helping to unpack the books. They called out to one another with delight as they discovered and opened each manuscript.

Ishaq watched them. How they burned with that fire!

As the scholars exclaimed over their discoveries, Ishaq saw his father making his way toward him. He too was holding a book, holding it gently. His eyes shone.

"I cannot be sure yet, I cannot be sure," he said to Ishaq. "But I believe this may be a book of Aristotle's that we have not yet seen. Please take it to my study so that we may examine it later."

Ishaq nodded and took the book, feeling the weight of it, feeling the age of it. He carried it to his father's study, and, placing it on the table, he turned to go.

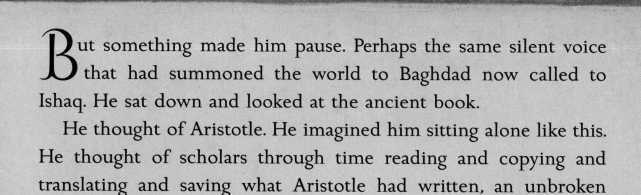

But something made him pause. Perhaps the same silent voice that had summoned the world to Baghdad now called to Ishaq. He sat down and looked at the ancient book.

He thought of Aristotle. He imagined him sitting alone like this. He thought of scholars through time reading and copying and translating and saving what Aristotle had written, an unbroken chain leading all the way to Baghdad, all the way to Ishaq, a thousand years later.

And then, lighting the lantern, he began to read.

As Ishaq read, he felt that Aristotle was in the room with him, was at his side, was speaking to him. He felt he was lighting a candle for him, a flame to guide him.

He did not notice that the moon had set, or that his father had looked in on him, had smiled and quietly closed the door.

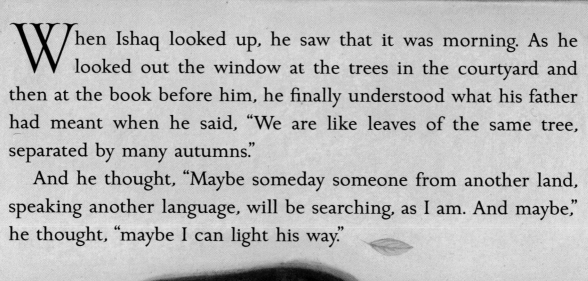

When Ishaq looked up, he saw that it was morning. As he looked out the window at the trees in the courtyard and then at the book before him, he finally understood what his father had meant when he said, "We are like leaves of the same tree, separated by many autumns."

And he thought, "Maybe someday someone from another land, speaking another language, will be searching, as I am. And maybe," he thought, "maybe I can light his way."

While Europe struggled darkly through poverty, ignorance, and superstition, the Arabic-speaking world was rediscovering the legacy of ancient Greece and had reached a level of civilization that Europe would not see for centuries. Not only was ninth-century Baghdad the capital of a vast empire, it was also the center of one of the world's greatest civilizations. From Morocco to Baghdad, the marks of advanced culture were evident: universities, hospitals, pharmacies, bookstores, banks, safe roads and highways.

In A.D. 830 the Caliph al-Ma'mun built an enormous edifice called *bayt al-hikmah*— the House of Wisdom—which was in fact a learning institution, a library, and a translation bureau. There, scholars preserved the great intellectual contributions of the ancient world. As these great minds of medieval Islam explored new horizons, they made invaluable contributions to medicine, astronomy, philosophy, history, geography, and mathematics. Among their many lasting achievements, they invented algebra, and it was in the observatory of the House of Wisdom that scholars determined the circumference of the earth.

Caliph al-Ma'mun, Hunayn, and Ishaq all played important parts in this period of enlightenment and contributed greatly to the sum of human knowledge: the Caliph as the founder of the House of Wisdom and a passionate patron of the sciences; Hunayn, whose noble example influenced many generations of scholars; and Ishaq, who would devote his life to translating the entire known body of Aristotle's work and would become the greatest translator of Aristotle who ever lived. Through their work, the scholars in the House of Wisdom introduced Greek thought to Europe, sparking the Renaissance. They carried the torch of civilization for the rest of the world.

WISDOM

We are like leaves of the same tree, separated by many autumns.

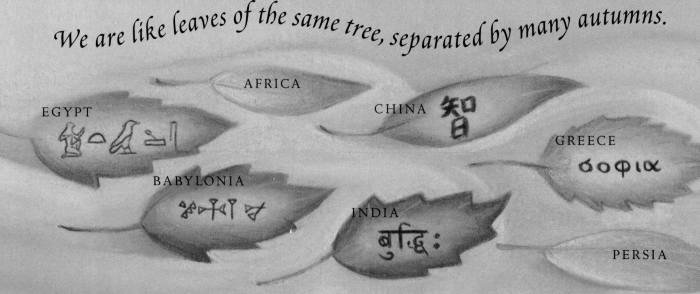

EGYPT

AFRICA

CHINA 智日

GREECE
σοφια

BABYLONIA

INDIA
बुद्धि:

PERSIA

3000 B.C.   2000 B.C.   1000 B.C.

ASIA

EUROPE

CHINA

★ BAGHDAD

ISLAMIC EMPIRE
AD 800

PERSIA

INDIA

AFRICA

N

W

E

S

ROME

Sapientia

BAGHDAD

الحكمة

THE RENAISSANCE

A.D. 1   A.D. 1000

To Melanie Kroupa and to all who search for wisdom and knowledge

F. P. H. & J. H. G.

To students of all ages~may you always be hungry for more

M. G.

Authors' Bibliography

Hourani, Albert
A History of the Arab Peoples
Warner Books, New York, 1991

Von Grunebaum, G. E.
Classical Islam
Aldine Publishing Co., Chicago, 1970

Peters, F. E.
Aristotle and the Arabs
New York University Press, New York,
1968

Hitti, Philip K.
History of the Arabs
MacMillan and Co., London, 1937

Lewis, Bernard
The Arabs in History
Harper & Row, New York, 1958

Gibb, Hamilton A. R.
Studies on the Civilization of Islam
Beacon Press, Boston, 1962

Rosenthal, Erwin I. J.
Political Thought in Medieval Islam
Cambridge University Press, London,
1958

Levy, Reuben
The Social Structure of Islam
Cambridge University Press, London,
1969

Nicholson, R. A.
A Literary History of the Arabs
Cambridge University Press, London,
1969

Brockelmann, Carl
History of the Islamic Peoples
Capricorn Books, New York, 1960

Fakhry, Majid
A History of Islamic Philosophy
Columbia University Press, New York,
1970

Wiet, Gaston
Baghdad: Metropolis of the Abbasid Caliphate
University of Oklahoma Press,
Norman, Oklahoma, 1971

Illustrator's Bibliography

Lewis, Bernard, editor
The World of Islam
Thames & Hudson, London, 1976

Michell, George, editor
Architecture of the Islamic World
Thames & Hudson, London, 1978

Petrosyan, Yuri A., editor
Pages of Perfection
ARCH Foundation, Lugano, 1995

Rahman, Fazlur
Islam
Doubleday Anchor, New York, 1966

A.D. 2000

Caliph al-Ma'mun (al ma MOON)

Hunayn (hoo NANE)

Ishaq (ISS hak)

bayt al-hikmah (bait al HICK ma)

al-hikmah—wisdom

A Melanie Kroupa Book

DK
Ink

DK Publishing, Inc.
95 Madison Avenue
New York, New York 10016

Visit us on the World Wide Web at http://www.dk.com

Library of Congress Cataloging-in-Publication Data

Heide, Florence Parry.
   The House of Wisdom / by Florence Parry Heide and Judith Heide Gilliland;
illustrated by Mary GrandPré. — 1st ed.
      p.   cm.
   Summary: Ishaq, the son of the chief translator to the Caliph of ancient
Baghdad, travels the world in search of precious books and manuscripts and
brings them back to the great library known as the House of Wisdom.
   ISBN 0-7894-2562-9
   [1. Books and reading — Fiction. 2. Libraries — Fiction.
3. Baghdad (Iraq) — Fiction.]
I. Gilliland, Judith Heide. II. GrandPré, Mary, ill. III. Title.
PZ7.H36Hn   1999   98-7375
[Fic]—dc21   CIP
   AC

Book design by Mary GrandPré and Chris Hammill Paul.
The text of this book is set in 15 point ITC Golden Cockerel.
The illustrations for this book were created with pastel.

Printed and bound in the United States of America
First Edition, 1999

2 4 6 8 10 9 7 5 3 1